Henrietta and the Hat

by Mabel Watts
illustrated by Ann Schweninger

MERRIGOLD PRESS • NEW YORK

One day Farmer Flinders bought a new hat.
It was a chocolate-colored hat with a band of
ribbon around it. A little red feather stuck up
on one side.

Henrietta the horse took a fancy to Farmer Flinders' hat. "That hat would look just right on me!" she thought. "I wish it were mine."

But Henrietta did not get the hat. She got a nice bag of oats every day, but not the chocolate-colored hat.

As time went on the sun shone down on the hat. The winds blew on it, the rains rained on it, and the snows snowed on it.

By and by the chocolate-colored hat began to look rather shabby. That was when Farmer Flinders gave the hat to Mrs. Flinders.

Mrs. Flinders wore the hat when she weeded the vegetable garden.

Henrietta saw the hat perched on Mrs. Flinders' head. It had faded. The ribbon was frayed, and the feather looked ragged. The brim was beginning to curl up at the edges.

But to Henrietta the chocolate-colored hat was still the most beautiful hat in the world. "Such a wonderful hat," she thought. "I wish it were mine!"

But Henrietta did not get the hat. She got a carrot every day, but not the chocolate-colored hat.

One day Mrs. Flinders saw herself in the mirror, wearing the hat. "Oh, dear," she said. "This hat is not the least bit becoming to me!"

She took off the hat and never put it on again. That was when Freddy Flinders began using the hat to gather eggs.

Freddy gathered lots and lots of eggs in the hat. Bantam eggs, medium-sized eggs, and large eggs. White eggs, speckled eggs, and brown eggs.

And every day Henrietta watched Freddy carry the hat, full of eggs, from the chicken coop to the kitchen door. "How truly lovely that hat would look on me," she thought. "I wish it were mine!"

But Henrietta did not get the hat. She got a pat on the back and a knob of sugar every day, but not the chocolate-colored hat.

One day...*spat!* An egg fell through the side of the hat. "There's a hole in this hat," Freddy said. "I can't use it for gathering eggs any more."

He left it lying under a tree. That was when a bird built her nest in the hat.

For days the bird flitted here and there, busily collecting leaves and grass and straw to line the hat.

Then she laid four pale blue eggs in it.

By this time the hat had grown flattish and floppy. But it still looked beautiful to Henrietta. "If only I had that hat," she thought, "I'd be the best-looking horse in the county!"

But Henrietta did not get the hat. She got a bed of sweet-smelling hay every night, but not the chocolate-colored hat.

The hat made a snug home for the baby birds that hatched from the pale blue eggs.

Every morning the mother bird fed her family. The baby birds grew and grew. They grew right out of the chocolate-colored hat and flew away.

Now the hat was drab and dusty, but to Henrietta it looked lovelier than ever.

One morning Farmer Flinders found the hat under the tree. "Look at this old thing," he said to Freddy. "It has *two* holes in it now, not just one."

Freddy looked at the two holes. Then he looked at Henrietta. He looked especially at her long ears.

That was when Freddy put the hat on Henrietta's head. Henrietta had waited a long time for the chocolate-colored hat, and now at last it was hers!

The chocolate-colored hat fit Henrietta
perfectly. She tossed her head and whinnied
her highest, happiest whinny.

Henrietta knew she was the best-looking horse in the county!